THANJAVU[R]

BUILT BY RAJA RAJA CHOLA I, THE BRIHADEESWARA TEMPLE TOWERS OVER THE HISTORIC TOWN OF THANJAVUR, IN THE HEART OF TAMIL NADU. FOR CENTURIES PEOPLE HAVE MARVELLED AT IT AND AT THE OTHER ARCHITECTURAL MASTERPIECES BUILT HERE BY VARIOUS CHOLA MONARCHS. THE MONUMENTS ARE STEEPED IN HISTORY AND MYTHOLOGY. OUR STORY GOES BACK TO THE BIRTH OF THANJAVUR.

ON THE BANKS OF THE RIVER KAVERI, LIVED A WICKED ASURA NAMED THANJAN. HE TERRORISED THE PEOPLE LIVING THERE.

HELP!

AAAAH!

SAVE US, LORD VISHNU!

UP IN DEVALOKA*–

WE MUST ASK LORD VISHNU TO DESTROY THE EVIL DEMON.

* THE ABODE OF THE GODS

THANJAN'S WISH WAS GRANTED AND THANJAVUR OR THANJAN'S UR* WAS BORN. POETS SANG PRAISES OF THE FERTILE LAND AND ITS WEALTHY PEOPLE.

THEY GET SO MUCH RICE FROM THEIR FIELDS THAT THEY USE ELEPHANTS INSTEAD OF OXEN TO THRESH THE PADDY.

THE WOMEN FLING THEIR HEAVY GOLD EARRINGS TO CHASE AWAY THE BIRDS THAT PECK AT THE GRAIN THEY PUT OUT TO DRY.

THANJAVUR BECAME THE CAPITAL OF THE CHOLA KINGS IN THE 9TH CENTURY CE. AROUND 945 CE, PARANTAKA SUNDARA CHOLA II RECEIVED HAPPY NEWS.

THE QUEEN HAS HAD A BABY BOY!

* UR MEANS PLACE AND IT IS PRONOUNCED 'OOR'.

WE SHALL NAME THE BABY ARULMOZHI VARMAN.

ONE WHOSE WORDS ARE PRECIOUS. WHAT A LOVELY NAME!

IT IS SAID THAT THE MANY WIVES OF THE SERPENT ADISESHA* DANCED WITH JOY AT PRINCE ARUL'S BIRTH.

HE WILL RELIEVE OUR HUSBAND OF CARRYING THE BURDEN OF THE EARTH!

PRINCE ARULMOZHI ASCENDED THE THRONE IN 985 CE.

THE RITUAL OF THE SACRED BATH IS OVER. YOU SHALL HENCEFORTH BE KNOWN AS RAJA RAJA, KING OF KINGS.

KING OF KINGS HE DID PROVE HIMSELF TO BE. FOR UNDER RAJA RAJA'S WISE AND MATURE LEADERSHIP, THE CHOLAS BECAME A GREAT POWER.

WE SHOULD GO TO WAR AT ONCE, O KING, AND CONQUER NEW TERRITORIES!

NO, WE MUST FIRST TRAIN OUR SOLDIERS AND CREATE A STRONG ARMY.

* ALSO KNOWN AS SHESHNAG, AND IS SAID TO SUPPORT THE EARTH ON ITS HOOD.

EIGHT YEARS WENT BY.

WE ARE READY FOR BATTLE! PREPARE TO LAUNCH AN ATTACK ON THE CHERA KING, BHASKARA RAVIVARMAN.

WE HAVE DESTROYED THE ENTIRE FLEET OF THE CHERAS!

WELL DONE!

RAJA RAJA SPENT THE NEXT FEW YEARS CONQUERING NEW TERRITORIES.

MY KINGDOM STRETCHES FROM CHERALAM* TO LANKA, AND FROM MUNNIR PALANTIVU PANNIRAYIRAM^ TO KALINGA^^.

THERE ARE MORE PRIZES TO BE WON, YOUR MAJESTY.

* KERALA   ^^ ORISSA
^ MALDIVES

NO, I HAVE HAD ENOUGH! I HAVE REALISED ALL MY MILITARY AMBITIONS. NOW I ONLY WISH TO SERVE LORD SHIVA, LIKE MY GRAND-AUNT SEMBIYAN MAHADEVI.

IT SHALL BE AS YOU WISH, YOUR MAJESTY.

IN HER TIME, SEMBIYAN MAHADEVI HAD BUILT MANY TEMPLES IN AND AROUND THANJAVUR. ONE OF THE TEMPLES WAS AT KONERIRAJAPURAM.

THE QUEEN WISHES TO INSTALL A BRONZE NATARAJA HERE. IT SHOULD BE AT LEAST 6 FEET TALL.

IT SHALL BE DONE, O KING!

LEGEND HAS IT THAT EVEN AFTER MANY ATTEMPTS –

WHAT IS THIS? ANOTHER SMALL STATUE?

I AM HELPLESS, SIRE, THE STATUE DOES NOT RISE BEYOND THAT.

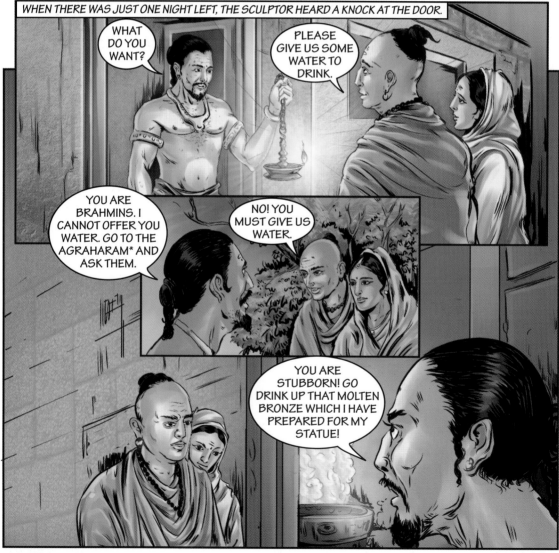

*BRAHMIN COLONY

THE NEXT MORNING –

BEAUTIFUL! WHAT WONDERFUL WORK!

IT WAS LORD SHIVA, SIRE! HE AND THE GODDESS CAME AND TRANSFORMED THEMSELVES INTO THESE STATUES.

WHAT RUBBISH!

ARE YOU SAYING THE STATUE IS ALIVE?

CLANG

BLOOD!

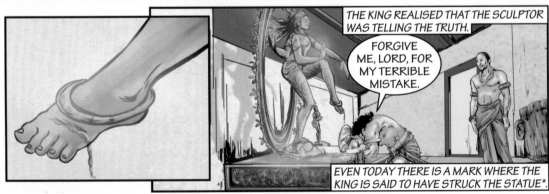

THE KING REALISED THAT THE SCULPTOR WAS TELLING THE TRUTH.

FORGIVE ME, LORD, FOR MY TERRIBLE MISTAKE.

EVEN TODAY THERE IS A MARK WHERE THE KING IS SAID TO HAVE STRUCK THE STATUE*.

* IT IS SAID TO BE THE WORLD'S TALLEST BRONZE NATARAJA.

*RELIGIOUS SONG

TO CHIDAMBARAM!

THE PALM LEAVES ON WHICH THE HYMNS ARE WRITTEN ARE IN A STORE ROOM AT THE BACK OF THE GOLDEN TEMPLE AT CHIDAMBARAM. THE ROOM HAS THE PALM IMPRINTS OF THE SAINTS ON ITS WALLS.

THIS IS THE ROOM WITH THE PALM IMPRINTS.

STOP! THE ROOM CAN ONLY BE OPENED IF YOU BRING THE THREE SAINTS HERE.

GRIEVE NOT, O KING! ONLY THOSE HYMNS FIT FOR THIS AGE ARE PRESERVED. THE REST HAVE BEEN CONSUMED AT MY WILL.

IT IS THE VOICE OF LORD SHIVA HIMSELF! I SHALL ARRANGE FOR THESE HYMNS TO BE COMPILED AND SUNG AT ALL SHIVA TEMPLES.

THE THEVARAM OR GARLAND OF HYMNS IS SUNG TO THIS DAY.

THE TEMPLE AUTHORITIES AT CHIDAMBARAM HONOURED THE KING.

FOR YOUR DEVOTION TO SHIVA WE CONFER ON YOU THE TITLE SRI RAJA RAJESWARA, GREATEST OF KINGS!

*TOWER

WHEN HE RECOVERED –

THIS IS WHERE I WILL BUILD THE SRI RAJA RAJESWARA TEMPLE*.

IT WILL BE FORTY TIMES LARGER AND FIVE TIMES TALLER THAN ANY OTHER TEMPLE. IT WILL BE MADE ENTIRELY OF GRANITE.

SIRE, THERE IS NO GRANITE QUARRY FOR MILES AROUND!

WE SHALL GET THE GRANITE FROM MAMMALAI.

BUT THAT IS ALMOST 30 MILES AWAY.

THAT DOES NOT MATTER. THE GRANITE WILL BE BROUGHT BY ROAD. BEGIN MAKING THE ROAD AT ONCE.

RAJA RAJA'S ENTHUSIASM WAS INFECTIOUS.

I WANT THE WHOLE TEMPLE COVERED WITH CARVINGS. CAN YOU CHISEL THE HARD GRANITE WITH YOUR SOFT IRON TOOLS?

YES! WE CAN!

* THE TEMPLE CAME TO BE KNOWN AS THE BRIHADEESWARA TEMPLE, POPULARLY CALLED THE BIG TEMPLE.

THE WORKERS SURPASSED THEMSELVES.

A BROOMSTICK CAN GO INTO EACH OF THE TINY HOLES WHICH ARE PLACED AT EQUAL DISTANCES.

WHAT GEOMETRIC PLANNING!

LOOK AT THE HORSE'S BRIDLE IN THIS PANEL. THE STONE IS CARVED TO LOOK LIKE A REAL ROPE.

THE 18-FOOT HIGH DWARAPALAKAS OR GATEKEEPERS ASTOUNDED ALL.

IT IS BIGGER THAN A FULL-GROWN ELEPHANT!

IT IS SAID THAT THE CAPSTONE OF THE TEMPLE WAS MADE OF A SINGLE STONE WHICH ORIGINALLY BELONGED TO A COWHERDESS.

I WISH I COULD GIVE THIS STONE TO THE BIG TEMPLE.

YOUR WISH SHALL BE COMMUNICATED TO THE KING.

DID THAT VOICE COME FROM HEAVEN?

THE CAPSTONE WAS READIED, AND THEN –

LET A LONG RAMP BE BUILT FROM THE WOMAN'S HOUSE TO THE TOP OF THE TEMPLE.

BRILLIANT IDEA! AND ELEPHANTS SHALL PULL THE STONE UP.

HOWEVER, IN REALITY THE CAPSTONE IS MADE OF SMALLER STONES PUT TOGETHER. WHAT IS AMAZING IS THAT THE STONES ARE HELD TOGETHER WITHOUT USING CEMENT OR ADHESIVE OF ANY KIND!

A HUGE STATUE OF NANDI STANDS AT THE ENTRANCE. THERE IS A STORY THAT ONCE RAJA RAJA STOOD QUIETLY WATCHING THE SCULPTOR AT WORK.

PREPARE ME A PAAN*, BOY.

AS THE SCULPTOR TURNED TO SPIT —

OH!

BRING ME THE SPITTOON, BOY!

FORGIVE ME, O KING.

RISE! IT IS MY PRIVILEGE TO SEE YOU CREATE SUCH A BEAUTIFUL NANDI.

*BETEL LEAF

I WANT YOU TO INSCRIBE ON THE WALLS A LIST OF THE GIFTS GIVEN BY ME, MY FAMILY AND MY PEOPLE TO THE TEMPLE.

THE INSCRIPTIONS GIVE DETAILS ABOUT THE REIGN OF THE CHOLAS.

THE TEMPLE WAS FINALLY COMPLETED IN 1010 CE.

TODAY, 25 YEARS AFTER BECOMING THE KING, I CONSECRATE THE BRIHADEESWARA TEMPLE WITH WATER FROM THE SACRED RIVERS.

RAJA RAJA CHOLA HAD ALSO ORDERED THE WALLS OF THE TEMPLE TO BE ADORNED WITH FRESCOES.

THE MOST MAGNIFICENT OF THESE PAINTINGS IS THAT OF SHIVA AS TRIPURANTAKA*.

THE STORY GOES THAT …

… ONCE, THREE ASURA BROTHERS, KAMARAKSHA, TAARAKAKSHA AND VIDYUNMALI PERFORMED INTENSE PENANCE TO BRAHMA. AFTER MANY YEARS, BRAHMA APPEARED TO GRANT THEM A BOON.

GRANT US THREE CITIES THAT CANNOT BE DESTROYED.

NOTHING LASTS FOREVER.

THEN LET IT BE THAT THEIR DESTRUCTION IS CAUSED ONLY BY A SINGLE ARROW.

THE THREE CITIES WILL BE IN DIFFERENT WORLDS AND MADE OF GOLD, SILVER AND IRON.

THEY WILL MEET ONLY ONCE IN A 1000 YEARS.

I GRANT YOUR WISH.

* THE FORM IN WHICH SHIVA DESTROYED TRIPURA

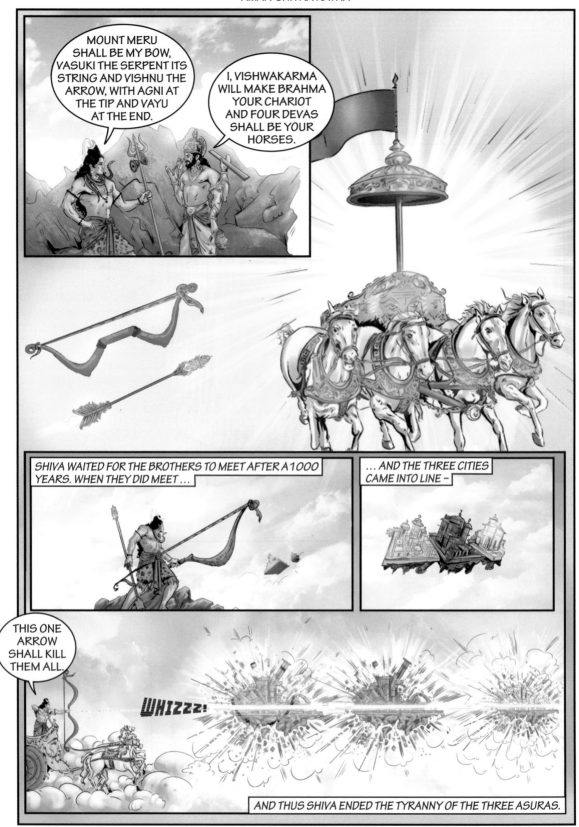

ANOTHER FRESCO TELLS THE STORY OF SUNDARAR, A SHAIVITE* SAINT.

SUNDARAR WAS THE ADOPTED SON OF THE CHIEF OF A LOCAL KINGDOM. AT HIS WEDDING –

STOP! THIS MAN SUNDARAR IS MY SLAVE. I HAVE THIS PALM SCRIPT SIGNED BY HIS FOREFATHERS TO PROVE IT.

SUNDARAR FOLLOWED THE OLD MAN TO A TEMPLE.

ALAS, SUNDARAR! WHAT THIS MAN SAYS IS TRUE. HE IS NOW YOUR MASTER.

ENOUGH CHATTER! NOW FOLLOW ME.

* FOLLOWER OF SHIVA

SUDDENLY –

HUH? WHERE DID HE GO?

I WAS THE OLD MAN, SUNDARAR. I HAVE CHOSEN YOU TO COMPOSE DEVOTIONAL SONGS FOR ME.

I AM HONOURED, O LORD!

SUNDARAR COMPOSED MANY SONGS AND WROTE ABOUT THE SHAIVITE SAINTS.

HE VISITED MANY PLACES, SINGING SHIVA'S PRAISES. ON ONE OF HIS TRAVELS, HE FELL IN LOVE WITH A WOMAN NAMED PARAVAYAR AND MARRIED HER.

WHEN RAJA RAJA DIED, HIS SON RAJENDRA CHOLA FURTHER EXPANDED THE EMPIRE.

WE CHOLAS ARE DESCENDANTS OF THE SUN. OUR LIGHT SHALL SPREAD ACROSS THE LAND. LET US MARCH NORTH!

YOU HAVE DEFEATED MANY KINGS ALL THE WAY UP NORTH TO THE GANGA*. YOU SHALL BE KNOWN AS GANGAI KONDA CHOLA OR THE CHOLA WHO TOOK THE GANGA.

I SHALL ESTABLISH A NEW CAPITAL HERE CALLED GANGAIKONDA CHOLAPURAM.

* THE RIVER GANGA

RAJENDRA CHOLA CONSTRUCTED A HUGE ARTIFICIAL LAKE AT GANGAIKONDA CHOLAPURAM.

I WANT THIS 'LIQUID PILLAR OF VICTORY' TO BE FILLED WITH WATER FROM THE HOLY GANGA BROUGHT HERE BY THE KINGS I HAVE DEFEATED.

HE ALSO BUILT A TEMPLE THERE.

THIS TEMPLE WILL BE BETTER THAN THE ONE MY FATHER BUILT. LET ALL THE MONEY AND THE GIFTS TO THE BRIHADEESWARA TEMPLE BE SHIFTED HERE.

UNDER RAJENDRA CHOLA, THE CHOLA EMPIRE REACHED ITS ZENITH, ITS INFLUENCE REACHING AS FAR AS DISTANT JAVA AND SUMATRA.

THOUGH THE CHOLA EMPIRE ENDED IN 1279 AD, THE MONUMENTS THEY BUILT IN AND AROUND THANJAVUR CONTINUE TO ENTHRALL THOUSANDS OF VISITORS FROM AROUND THE WORLD.

MORE ABOUT THANJAVUR

THE MARATHAS AND THE NAYAKS WHO RULED THANJAVUR IN THE MEDIEVAL PERIOD CONTRIBUTED GREATLY TO ITS RICH HERITAGE. THE SUBRAMANYA SHRINE IN THE BRIHADEESWARA TEMPLE COMPLEX HAS A PORTRAIT GALLERY OF THE MARATHA RULERS OF THANJAVUR.

THANJAVUR PAINTINGS ARE FAMOUS FOR THEIR UNIQUE STYLE. EARLIER, STRIPS OF REAL GOLD AND GEMS WERE USED IN THE PAINTINGS.

THANJAVUR IS ALSO KNOWN FOR ITS BRONZE SCULPTURES. THESE CAN BE SEEN IN THE ART VILLAGE WHERE THEY ARE MADE USING TRADITIONAL METHODS.

THE RAJAGOPALA CANNON IN THANJAVUR IS ONE OF THE WORLD'S LARGEST AND LONGEST GUNS. THIS CANNON WAS CALLED THE AGNIYANTRA OR FIRE-BREATHING WEAPON IN MARATHA TIMES. IT WAS MADE IN THE 1600S DURING THE REIGN OF RAGUNATHA NAYAK AND HAS NEVER BEEN MOVED FROM WHERE IT WAS ORIGINALLY PLACED! DESPITE BEING IN THE OPEN THE CANNON HAS NOT RUSTED.

IN 1931, S.K. GOVINDASWAMI, A YOUNG LECTURER, WAS EXPLORING THE DARK NARROW PASSAGE SURROUNDING THE SANCTUM OF THE BRIHADEESWARA TEMPLE WHEN HE FOUND SOMETHING BENEATH THE CRACKED PLASTER OF THE WALLS. IT WAS THE CHOLA FRESCOES WHICH HAD BEEN HIDDEN FROM SIGHT FOR HUNDREDS OF YEARS!

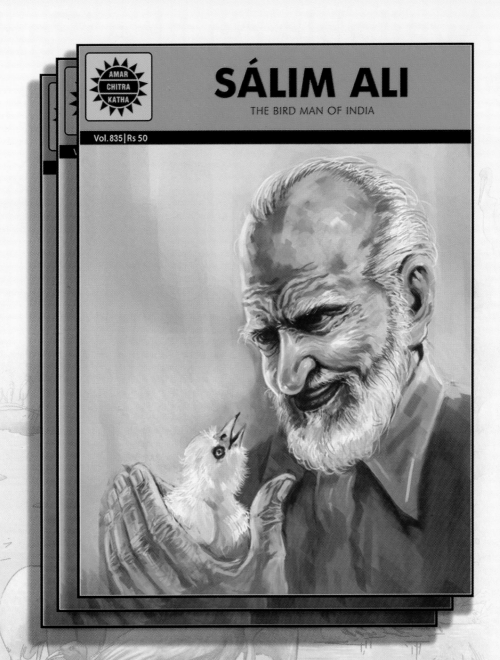

SÁLIM ALI
THE BIRD MAN OF INDIA

Vol. 835 | Rs 50

Available on the iPad!

A chemical engineer by profession, Anant Pai gave up his job to follow his dream, a dream that led to the birth of Amar Chitra Katha and Tinkle.

Anant Pai - Master Storyteller traces the story of the man who left behind a legacy of learning and laughter for children. ACK Media's new iPad app brings alive a new reading experience using panel-by-panel view technology, created in-house.